## Author/Illustrator: Kate Lupine

Kate Lupine's first Children's Book "Learning Lots About Lobsters" was a project she started in 2022 inspired by the hardworking Lobsterman and women in her community. The intention of this book is meant to present fun facts about Lobsters, while also giving a favorable nod to the Lobstering community of Maine.

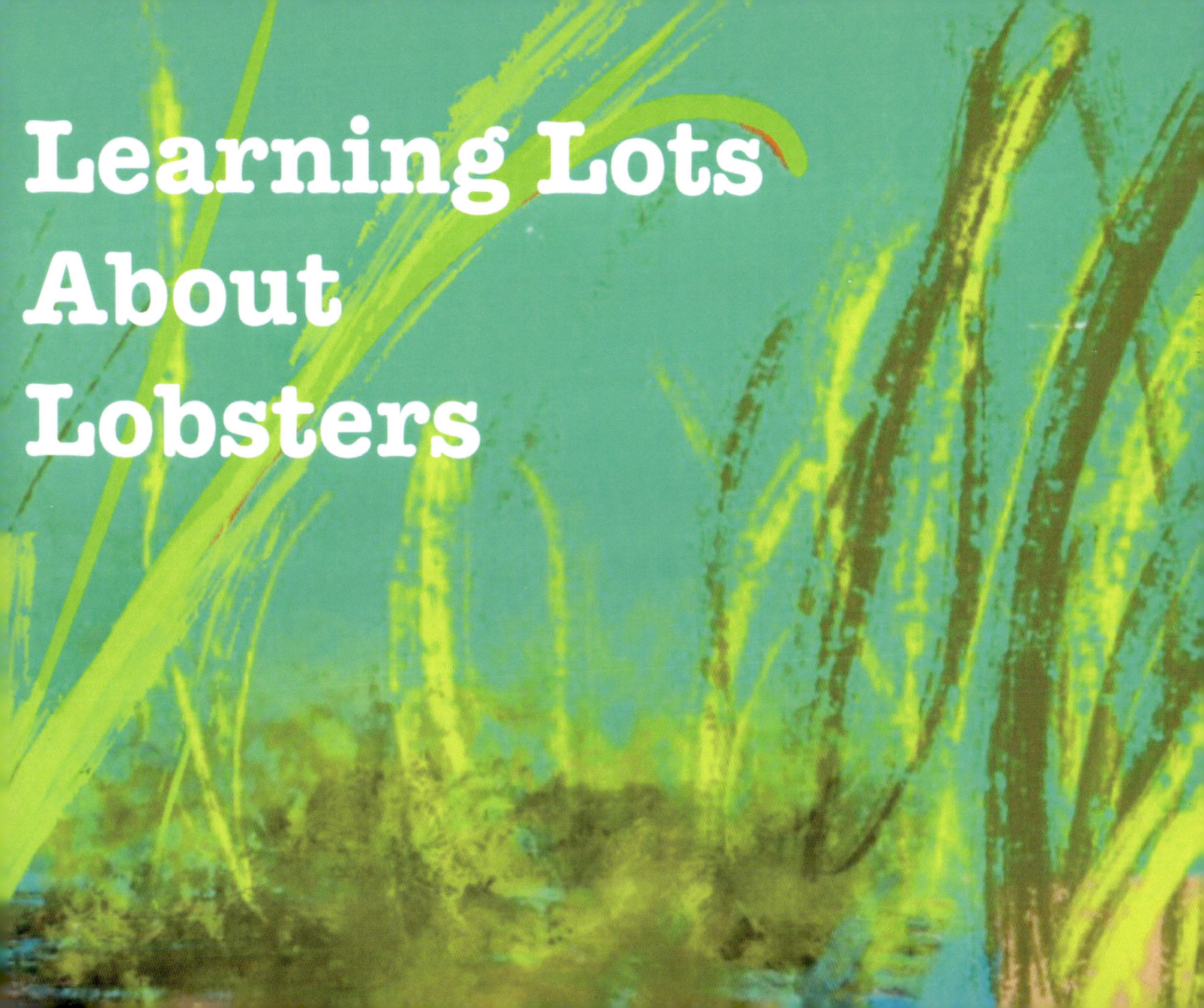
# Learning Lots About Lobsters

**Lobsters live in the salty waters of the sea.**

In the coldest of temperatures...

they are happy as can be!

As lobsters grow their shells become uncomfortable and tight.

When the time is right...

**Crabs**

When they want to move about,
they scoot around with their tails.

they will be thrown back
so they can strengthen the pod.

# Bibliography

Admin. 10 Facts You Do Not Know about Lobsters, 5 Sept. 2019, https://www.lobster88.com/2019/09/05/10-fact-lobster/.

Arthur, Charles. Reference Photograph. June 2022. Accessed December 2022

"Questions from Kids about Lobsters & Lobstering - Lobster Institute - University of Maine." Lobster Institute, https://umaine.edu/lobsterinstitute/educational-resources/lobsters/.

Weathervane, Admin. "When Is Lobster Season? Here's What to Know & When to Eat!" Weathervane Seafood Restaurants, 26 Jan. 2018, https://weathervaneseafoods.com/lobster-best-time-to-buy-all-year-long-at-weathervane/.

# Special Thanks

To my parents for all of their love and support. Additionally, to my Dad, Chris Kirby, for his editing assistance.

DEC 20 2023